DR. PEANUT BOOK #1

Nutty to Meet You!

BY ALAN VENABLE

PICTURES BY NATALIE LEWELLYN

ONE MONKEY BOOKS

San Francisco

OneMonkeyBooks.com

In memory of
Stephen ("Vince Poixnoix") Vance,
peanut friend and father

Published 2008 by
One Monkey Books
OneMonkeyBooks.com
156 Diamond Street
San Francisco, California
94114-2414

Book design by Susan G. Schroeder

ISBN: 978-0-9777082-0-8

10 9 8 7 6 5 4 3 2 1

If you ever meet Dr. Peanut, he will hold up his hand and say, "Nutty to meet you!"

Then you can say, "Nutty to meet you, too."

You could say *"Nice* to meet you," instead. But why not speak like the Talking Peanuts? How do they speak?

They speak in *Pinglish*.

Dr. Peanut is a doctor who looks after the Talking Peanut kids. In *Pinglish,* he is called a peanutrician.

Dr. Peanut likes his work. He likes to keep young Peanuts healthy. He taps their shells and tells them, "You sound nice and nutty today!"

Whenever a Peanut kid catches cold, Dr. Peanut is there with a hanky and a spoonful of syrup.

"Blow hard!" the doctor says.

Dr. Peanut lives a nutty life. But he does have one big problem.

He needs to be careful when he goes out.

He needs to stay out of sight of the giants.

Why?

Because giants eat peanuts!

Talking Peanuts wear disguises so that giants won't want to eat them.

Sometimes they disguise themselves as fallen leaves. (Most giants don't eat fallen leaves.)

Sometimes they disguise themselves as mice. (Most giants don't eat mice.)

One day, Dr. Peanut disguises himself as an ant. (Most giants don't eat ants.) He goes for a stroll in the park.

But squirrels in the park eat peanuts!

Dr. Peanut hurries around a tree and crawls inside a candy wrapper to hide until the squirrel is gone.

A giant hand comes down and scoops him up!
"Wait!" says the doctor.

"Did someone say something?" asks the giant.

"I said wait!"

"For what?" another giant asks. "Speak louder. We can barely hear you."

"Wait before you eat me!"

"Eat you?" says the giant boy. "Why would we eat you? You're not a candy bar."

"No, I'm an ant."

The giants look like they don't believe him. They don't look fooled by his disguise.

"Isn't it time for a snack?" asks the girl.

Dr. Peanut needs to think fast to keep from being eaten!

"Young giants," he says, "you should not just pick things up in the park. You must never eat things that you find on the ground."

"We find strawberries on the ground," says the girl. "That's where they grow. And we eat *them.*"

"That's different," the doctor replies. "And never, ever eat ants!"

"Some people eat ants," says the boy. "But you're no ant."

"Oh no? What am I, then?"

Dr. Peanut hopes they think he is *some* kind of bug.

"You're a peanut."

"No, I'm not!"

"You are."

"Okay, maybe I am," says Dr. Peanut. "But I am also a doctor. Let me check to see if you are healthy. Please stick out your tongues and say, 'Ahhh.'"

"Ahhh," say the giants.

"Well," says the doctor, "you both look nutty to me, but you might get sick if you eat between meals."

"Is that really true?" asks the boy.

"Maybe not," says Dr. Peanut. "But you could be allergic to peanuts. If you are, the smallest taste of me could make you very ill!"

"We're not allergic," says the girl. "We eat peanut butter all the time."

"And chocolate covered peanuts," says the boy. They rub their tummies.

Things don't look good for Dr. Peanut. He sees himself being roasted and ground into butter and spread on a slice of bread. He sees himself covered in chocolate. He must think of something quick!

I know, he thinks. *I'll ask them to think how they would feel if they were I!*

"Tell me," he says, "how would *you* feel if someone cracked *your* shell?"

"Cracked our what?" asks the girl.

The boy laughs. "Do you think we're going to eat you?"

"Aren't you?"

The boy makes a face. "I don't eat anything that talks!"

"Me, neither," says the girl.

The doctor feels much better now.

He says, "Then would you mind taking me home?

That squirrel looks hungry."

"What made you dress up like an ant?" the girl asks as they carry the doctor home. "Is this the Peanuts' Halloween?"

"No," he says. "We Talking Peanuts wear disguises all the time. You should see me in my beetle costume."

The girl laughs. "You're nutty," she says.

Dr. Peanut smiles. "Thank you, my dear. You speak good *Pinglish!*"

"I have a nutty idea," says the boy. "Why don't you carry a megaphone? Here, I'll roll one out of paper. Then the giants will hear you better."

The doctor tries the megaphone.

"WOW," he says. His voice is much louder. **"WHAT A BRILLIANT IDEA!"**

"THAT'S WHERE I LIVE."

Dr. Peanut shakes hands with the giants. **"NUTTY TO MEET YOU,"** he says.

"Nutty to meet you, too!" they reply.

"I WOULD INVITE YOU IN," says the doctor,
"BUT I DON'T THINK YOU WOULD FIT."

"That's all right," they say. "You can come to our place.
See you soon."

Now Dr. Peanut has fewer problems out of doors.

He often goes out with his giants.

Sometimes they make a play date.

Wherever giants are around,

he always takes his megaphone...

...to let them know he's a Talking Peanut!